THE LAND OF BEARS

SHO]

BY

MAYA HORNICK

Short story 1 – Bearing Up Well.

Zagreb 1950

The boarding school is cold. At night I have to put a spare mattress over me to keep warm. All the other girls in the dormitory keep me awake with their snoring. I'm reading *War and Peace*, in Russian. After they have all gone to bed, I sometimes sneak into the bathroom, put the light on, shut the door and resume my reading. By summer I hope to finish the book and start on *Huckleberry Finn*.

The food is very spare. We are woken at 6am and taken outside to exercise, in all weathers.

After one hour of this we are given our daily disgusting dose of cod liver oil. I usually pour my portion and all the other girls' doses into the large plant pot I sit beside at the table. Nobody in their right mind would want to drink this pungent-smelling stuff that has the texture of slime. Then after that it's a breakfast of porridge and one piece of fruit. The portions are small. Most of us are very skinny and in all the years I've been here, I've never once had a cold nor heard of anyone else who had one. Keeping us lean and hungry all the time has some beneficial effect on our health. Once, however, I did spend a night in the sanatorium because of an allergy to strawberries – an itchy rash all over my back. It went away after a few days. I'd been disappointed because I missed that week's free classical music concert at the local concert hall in Zagreb.

What would happen is that if not enough tickets were sold by the date of the performance, some representative of the music venue would arrive at the school with lots of free tickets for the girls, so we could enjoy the concert while filling up seats. It was the highlight of my week, particularly if Mozart was on the bill. I was very studious but a bit of a loner, always up in my head in my own world. On the way to the concert I was often teased by boys who would shout out to me: "What's life like there up in the clouds?" or, "What's it like to be a giraffe?" You see, I was exceptionally tall for my age. I even had to have my shoes and clothes custom-made for me. At five foot eleven inches high and with size 9 feet, and still growing, I stood out from the crowd, literally.

I was one of the academic girls the others looked up to, but I'd rather they had not. I was often asked by teachers to oversee a class of girls and teach them, while the staff went on a very long lunch or tea break. Being very good at different subjects had its disadvantages. I had to spend many extra hours coaching students that lagged behind. This was nerve-wracking when it came to exam time as I was eager for my charges to perform well, or I might be blamed for being lazy at teaching them correctly. It added to the stress of an already stressful situation. Being away from home, with the exception of the summer months, was very lonely at times.

One afternoon when I was sent alone a few streets away to pick up something from a shop for one of the teachers, I noticed a new arrival in the big square of the old town, by St Mark's Church. There was a man with a bear. Yes, a performing bear tied to a post with a chain. The animal was very thin and seemed to me to have a woeful expression on its face. I felt very sorry for it. I wished I could set it free. The man, the owner, was probably a gypsy. He was singing as the bear danced and asking people passing by on the way to the market and elsewhere to spare a few dinars for him. I felt equally sorry for this man who was forced to do this to earn some money to survive. I was lucky that I had the opportunity to study to get into university. There was no question that I wouldn't do this. In my mother's day, opportunities like this for women were unheard of. She still wasn't able to read or write and didn't want to learn even though I offered to teach her.

The heat of the sun was beating down, the bear was lumbering about in some kind of a trance. Maybe he was given some sedative herbs to make him more obedient. Then for a few moments I blacked out and wasn't aware of my surroundings. When I re-engaged with reality once more, the bear and the man were gone and I wondered if the heat had made me hallucinate them in the first place. I felt weak and shaky but everything was as it had been. People were milling about as normal, minding their own business or stopping for a chat with someone they knew. Zagreb was a small town in which everyone seemed to know everyone else.

I hurried back to the school with the package for the teacher. She saw I was looking extremely pale and sent me to the sanatorium. Two times in one month! This was too much. My temperature was high. The nurse gave me a bitter liquid to bring the offending fever down. I had a night of delirium: a gypsy man trying to get me to dance when my feet were so sore; a bear stroking my forehead and saying soothing words as I lay in bed; dancing bears in a sky of sapphire blue and my mother singing to me the lullaby she sang to me when I was a very young child. All these images merged and shifted over one another in a dizzying display.

I woke the next day to great relief that I felt delirious no more. The nurse was asleep and snoring in her chair. I heard some tapping at the window and turned to see the bear looking in the window at me, smiling. Oh no, I think to myself, I must still be asleep. I shake my head to rid myself of this dream-like image but it still remains. I pinch myself several times but I don't wake up because I am awake. I take a deep breath and have another look. The bear is still there, head to one side, looking at me curiously.

"Shoo! Shoo!" I say, in an effort to scare him away. If he is found here, there is no knowing what would happen. I can only reason that he must have broken free of his tether and the gypsy man too for he is not about in the forecourt. How the bear got beyond the gates of the school, I don't know. I try to keep level-headed but my thoughts spin, trying to piece everything together. Is the bear real or just from my imagination? Have the herbs I was given to reduce the fever accidentally triggered my imagination to hallucinate? I feel a little anxious but decide not to tell anyone what I have been seeing.

I am allowed to join the girls for lunch as my fever has gone. The bear lumbers in and sits beside me where a girl has already finished and left. To my astonishment nobody mentions him at all. I feed him half of my lunch. He looks like he hasn't eaten in days. I wasn't very hungry anyway. He is very grateful.

Before my eyes he seems to blossom in strength. His eyes that previously were dull now become shiny and kind. His nose is now jet-black and moist and not pale grey anymore. And his muscles seem stronger. His power is returning to him. His fur is now lustrous and sleek like velvet and no more the matted terrible mess of scars and tufts it had been before. I only wish this lunch of unidentifiable stew and bread could have done the same for me. I am still feeling a little weak.

I am excused from classes for the afternoon and told to go to the dormitory in a nearby building and rest. As I walk across the street the bear holds my hand and makes sure I cross the road safely. The pads of his hand feel warm and smooth and soft – not so different from human hands. Nearing the dorm building I feel so sleepy that the bear lies down and asks me to climb on his back. (Yes, he actually spoke. It was a deep, gruff voice that sounded like the ancient forest speaking.) He swiftly ascends the steps to the room and gently deposits me on the bed, before tucking me in.

When I wake, it is night-time and all the girls lie in their beds asleep. I can see their shadowy silhouettes by the light of the moon. Stars shine down. There seem to be about a hundred million of them, blinking and trembling at me. My bear is beside me on the floor, eating a biscuit and drinking tea from a cup and saucer that are balanced on his tummy. They rattle as he breathes in and out.

"Well I thought I might as well," he says. "You were asleep. One of the girls left it for you. I didn't like it to go to waste."

"No, you go ahead. Feel free," I say, realising how strange it is to be talking to a bear in this way. What would my mother and younger brother think of all this?

"I do feel free, very free indeed," he replies. "Since you looked me in the eyes with such compassion at the town square, something inside me was untethered. I think it was my pain. It flowed out of me and drained away. Then I felt strong, like I could escape. You gave me courage once again."

"I'm glad," I whisper, for one of the girls was stirring in her sleep. "Why can't anybody see you but me?"

"Oh, but they can see me. They just don't believe I'm real, so they keep quiet and pretend I'm not here. You're the only one who believes I might really exist."

The next morning the bear is gone. I feel disappointed. At breakfast I'm handed a letter from my mother. She has heard about the strawberry rash episode and asks if I'm well. My brother has written it for her. I recognise his handwriting. I have some free time before lunch and I go to the music room to write a reply. But the music room is occupied. An older girl called Maya is playing the violin. It's so beautiful. I long to stay and listen but we're not allowed to loiter in the corridors. I vow that one day if I have a daughter of my own, I will call her Maya. And I will encourage her to play the violin.

I find a bench outside and write: "Dear mother, I'm bearing up well under the circumstances." And then I draw a picture of my bear as the nurse putting ointment on my back. I tell her everything is fine and to leave some food for the bears in the forest by the lakes so they don't come up to the village and get shot or manacled. I make a request to a teacher to be allowed to post the letter.

"I suppose the walk will do you some good," says the stern schoolmistress taking her break under the sheltering tree. I walk around the corner and three blocks down to post the letter. On my return, two boys from last week are over the road and they start jeering at me and making fun of my height. I slouch down and try to make myself look smaller. Then one tosses an apple at me. Before it hits my head I see a paw snatch it away. It is my bear again and he's beside me. He chomps on the apple while spitting and snarling at the boys. They yelp and run for their lives.

"They won't be messing with you again," says the bear.

"Isn't it about time I gave you a name?" I ask. "You seem to be sticking around, for now at least."

"My name is possibly "Dance! Dance!" or "Over here, you lumbering idiot!" The bear sounds doleful. He clearly doesn't like the sound of those names.

"Those weren't names, they were commands, ugly commands," I tell him and stroke his back. "I will call you Ivan, after the bear in the lullaby my mother used to sing to me whenever I was ill in bed."

"Ivan is a good strong name, thank you," says the bear.

He leaves me at the school gate and tells me I will be fine from now on and he will be fine too, now he has a good name to make him feel as strong as many bears all in one body.

As I grow up, the memories of the bear gradually fade from my mind and I wonder if it wasn't some fanciful invention created by a feverish brain. Sixty-five years later I am back in Zagreb on a holiday with my two children, now fully grown. I am showing them the boarding school where I spent so much time. None of the buildings have changed, but the walls have a fresh coat of yellow paint. It's a very hot day. The sun beats down and we head to St Mark's Church. All is as it was that day. People mill about in the heat, slowly. They look ancient and could even be the same people I saw before, all those years ago.

My daughter feels faint so I send my son to the shop on the corner to buy drinks and ice-lollies. She sits on some steps in the shade to cool down. Then I hear a voice, as deep and as ancient as the forest.

"It is hot out here, take care of yourselves. Leave the Old Town via the cooling steps by the park. Do not go the other way. Do not be afraid. Your daughter will recover. Tell her to leave some flowers by the stray grey cat sunning itself on the wall that she'll pass on the way down. The cat is not what it seems. It will bring luck." I turn and look everywhere for Ivan, my bear who springs back into my mind's eye. He is nowhere to be seen. But I notice an old man, stooped and with a stick, sitting by some paintings of Zagreb's landmarks that are for sale. I take a closer look and in each one is a bear that looks like Ivan. He is seeing the sights and enjoying them. It looks as if one other person could see him after all, and believed he was real.

The cat is indeed where the old man promised. My daughter leaves some pink flowers she bought from a flower seller by the park. The cat nods its head and purrs. It is to be the last time I visit Zagreb and I haven't heard nor seen anything of my bear since then. But I feel his strong presence sometimes, when I sense I'm in some kind of danger and it gives me added courage.

My daughter, who I did name Maya, paints pictures of animals. One day I ask her to paint me a bear in her usual colourful style. When she hands me the completed picture, I gasp. It is my bear, Ivan, even though I have never spoken to her about it. This is purely from her imagination. I pay her for the picture but tell her to keep it. I feel sure that it will bring her luck, and function like a protective talisman.

Sometimes when I dream, I hear Ivan's voice, soft and deep and low saying soothing words or telling me of his adventures. I usually wake up laughing because the stories are so funny. I wish I could tell stories as well as he does, but I leave that to my daughter who is also a writer. Perhaps sometime in the future she will hear Ivan's voice too and she can be able to channel his tales into books and out into the world. A series of children's books about a child who befriends a bear could be very amusing indeed. However, I think Paddington might mind. Or Winnie the Pooh. But then I also think to myself, there can never be too many good and funny bears in the world, not a world like ours that has so much sorrow.

I put on the radio and listen to Mozart. He is still my favourite composer. I imagine I am a child once more, in the concert hall in Zagreb, so many years ago. Transported to a different time and place in 18th century Vienna. Beside me in the aisle is Ivan, wearing a colourful cravat. He taps along to the music with his paws. He looks older now. His hair is greying and his jowls droop a little. He gets up and turns to me and says goodbye before walking up to the stage. As he does so, he transforms into a man who turns to me, smiles warmly and waves before disappearing into a mist. It's just like the mist that used to surround us in the forest near my mother's home by the lakes.

Although I have not seen him since I was three years old, because he died in the war, the man I have just seen is unmistakable. He is my father. I wake from my small daydream to find I am in my small cosy room in North London. Our cat lies curled up asleep on the bed and to my left on my writing bureau is an old, faded photograph of my dad. When I used to look at this image of him, I saw a man fixed in time at a particular point in history. Someone I could no longer reach or communicate with. Now I see him as someone who can travel through my dreams and memories, who has been guiding me and caring for me all along.

That lucky grey cat in Zagreb that my daughter left some flowers for did indeed turn out to be fortunate. On our return to London, some months later, my daughter bought a scratch card lottery ticket with a 'Lucky Cat' symbol on the front and won £10,000. She always wanted to visit Venice and now we'll have the chance. I wonder what new stories she will come up with after our trip. Father would be pleased she is getting to fulfil one of her dreams, even if he is no longer here in person to see it. But here in spirit, he most definitely is.

Short story 2 – The Land of Bears and Wolves

Plitvice Lakes National Park, 2011

I put on my walking shoes and go downstairs. The smell of freshly-made scrambled eggs and toast wafts up to greet me as I descend the steps to the dining area of the guesthouse. The other visitors have already eaten and left, I'm told. Katya is looking after the guesthouse for her son, the owner. She makes the best scrambled eggs I've ever tasted. The eggs have been laid this morning in the chicken coup round the back and the cheese she adds is made in the village from local cows. There is just the right amount of salt and pepper to taste.

Coffee is of the freshly ground variety. Katya has a bronze hand-mill for the purpose, the same kind my grandmother would've used, back in the day. My Grandmother lived in Plitvice and Katya is an old friend of the family.

For some reason I hadn't slept well despite the comfortable bed and air conditioning. I was restless, and possibly excited about the day ahead. I haven't visited the lakes since I was a child. Then, I'd been with family, traipsing through the forest near our family home, picking wild strawberries from the path along the way. We sat at the lakeside and played with autumn leaves and drank straight from the lake, its crystal pure liquid, cold and refreshing, before returning to the house and the attendant mosquitoes. Strangely enough, I was never bothered by any of the mosquitoes in the forest, not even by the lake.

I sip my coffee and wonder how long the walk will be to the entrance of the national park. Katya doesn't speak much English and my Croatian is very patchy. I ought to have made more of an effort to learn some of the language but somehow other things had gotten in the way.

Back in my room, I check I have everything in my backpack ready for the day. I will pick up some fruit and other edible supplies for the journey from the small supermarket en route. I wave Katya goodbye. "Stick to the path," she calls out as I leave. I'd heard that landmines were still to be found in some areas, from the homeland war. I wasn't planning on stepping on one any time soon, or any time at all, for that matter.

Beyond the supermarket there is a downhill slope with a pine tree forest on each side, and a rough dirt path in the centre. It's cooler here than out in the open. The trees give off a scent that reminds me of my childhood: woody, earthy, and minty. Breathing in deeply, I feel invigorated. Kicking up the dirt as I walk, there's a gathering of brown dust in my wake like clouds. A slight mist is among the trees, swirling around the trunks and branches like a semi-opaque seductive scarf. That mist was known to my grandmother to possess an evil miasma that laid her up in bed with pneumonia one whole summer long ago. She always warned me about that mist, how never to go walking into the forest when it was there. She'd given me a lucky charm to help me find my way home if I ever got lost in the woods. I tied it to my belt this morning, just to be on the safe side.

A German couple, talking excitedly, pass by. They are sparing no time at all in reaching the lakes. I, however, am a little more sedate. I want to meditate on the beauty and peace of the wood as I pass through it, and not let my thoughts run on ahead of my steps. As I progress down the path, the trees seem more dense and enclosing. Sunlight filters through in a soft haze but shadows are everywhere nonetheless. The path goes on and on, descending deeper. The gentle rhythm of my steps lulls me into a state of trance-like stillness. I listen for birdsong but there's none.

In my ears is the sound of my heart loudly beating. Then there's the slow hiss of my breath every time I exhale. I feel stronger somehow, as if I have taken on larger dimensions. I stumble and reach out to steady myself even though there's nothing on the path to hold onto. I gasp. My arm isn't my own arm anymore, but that of a bear. I raise my hands up to my face, but they are paws with claws now. I gently feel my nose, which is no longer an upturned little button-like fixture, but a snout. I look down at my body. My clothes are all gone, and I now have the body of a bear. It's no longer comfortable to stand upright and so I get down on all fours and lumber forward as if some instinct for survival guides me.

I hear voices behind me, shouting, coming closer. I run and run, knowing humans are to be feared. But I'm not fast enough. Gunshots ring out and there is a searing pain in my leg. I am limping now but terror and adrenalin kick in and so I move faster. I diverge from the path and run into the forest. I want to scream but only a loud growl-like thunder leaves my mouth. I run so fast and for so long that I think that surely I will reach the lakes, but the wood grows denser until I'm utterly lost and the shouts of the pursuers become more muffled until they eventually stop.

I sit down against a tree and close my eyes. There's lots of birdsong now, a cacophony that assails me from all directions. Then snarling begins. My eyes are wide open now. Wolves, lean and hungry, close in. One lunges at me, jaws wide, saliva drooling. Then another and another follow in a frenzied attack. With my animal might I slash at them with my claws. One after another they

23

crash to the ground, wounded and whimpering. But I don't see the one poised in the tree above me ready to strike – a fatal bite, wolf-jaws clamping down on my neck. My vision fades and all goes dark as I slip into unconsciousness.

Someone is saying my name, soft and low, over and over, like a prayer. I feel dizzy and bruised but gradually the image of the wolves leaves my retina and my room at the guesthouse appears before me. I am lying on the bed. Katya is beside me holding my hand. The doctor has been already and pronounced that I passed out on the path. According to Katya, he said I must've had a panic attack and fainted. I feel the back of my head where there is now a lovely bump, very sore to touch. My bear's body has been left behind and I am clothed again in my shorts and T-shirt. Only my shoes have been removed and lie beside my backpack on the floor.

The doctor found an odd circular bruise on the back and front of my calf, each the size and shape of a bullet hole. I decide to tell no one of my strange vision, if that's what it was. I am instructed to rest and visit the lakes the next day instead. To not go via the path in the woods but get a lift in the car to the main entrance from Katya's son Tommy who has arrived home with his family from a holiday by the sea. I am grateful for their concern but really I feel it's a lot of fuss about nothing. Still, I don't want to go down that particular path again any time soon. Not with the misty miasma my grandmother spoke about. It probably got into my lungs, affecting my brain, causing hallucinations. I reach for the lucky charm attached to my belt. To my relief it's still there. My wish to explore the lakes hasn't diminished. I will rest, gather my strength, and embark on a new adventure tomorrow.

*

The next morning I shower and notice that the bruise on my leg that was so prominent last night has gone. At breakfast I see the German couple from yesterday at the next table. The lady smiles at me and there's a tinge of pity in her expression. Katya isn't here today. I ask Tommy's wife, Anna, where she is but she just shrugs and says she went to visit a friend in the next village and doesn't know when she'll be back.

My appetite is diminished from the stress of yesterday's strange visions so I leave breakfast half-finished. The previous night I slept badly, dreaming that I was fleeing something threatening that was chasing me downhill.

Upstairs in my room I prepare my backpack, checking everything I need is there. I reach for my straw hat on the bedside cabinet and hurry downstairs. Tommy is waiting outside leaning against his car, smoking a cigarette. He glances at me but carries on as before, leisurely taking drag after drag. "We leave in moment," he commands, unsmiling, brushing a mosquito from his arm, and letting the cigarette ash fall on the parched turf. He finishes the last long drag and stubs out his 'death stick', as my grandma used to call them, on the turf.

Finally Tommy gestures for me to get in. Soon we're gliding over the gravelly path, small stones flying up and hitting the car. The road is a convoluted path to the side of the wood and as we go by I notice that the mist of yesterday hasn't prevailed. The forest looks benign with no hint of wolves or bears or of people in pursuit. I wonder if the events I witnessed the day before were all a dream brought on by the heat but I choose to keep an open mind about it. A friend studying philosophy once told me that the world could be composed of multiple realities at play, laid over each other like Russian dolls. Sometimes, he said, certain individuals develop the ability to travel between these different worlds. I'd dismissed it at the time as absurd but now I wasn't so sure.

At the bottom of the hill by the entrance to the lakes Tommy drops me off and says he will be back at 6pm to pick me up. There is a notice saying that bathing in the lakes is strictly forbidden.

People are milling about trying to get into the queue for the bus that will take them to the top of the lakes. It's a 10-minute bus ride to our destination, passing by pine woodland. Once there we get our day passes and embark on walking along the designated path. The visitors set off at a fast pace leaving me trailing behind.

Over the lakes is a wooden walkway made with slats through which I can see the water below. The soothing blue colour is so welcoming and the water so clear that I have frequent impulses to dive in. The lake I'm travelling over is vast and wide. In the silence it's like a vision to behold. It seems unreal, it's so beautiful. Turquoise dragonflies flit about the reeds. I hear the gentle vibration of their wings.

After some time I stop and have a drink, taking in the view. Lakes surrounded by forests on all sides, clear blue sky, and the water below beckoning to me with its bright hopeful stillness and promise of cooling touch. There are few people about now. I take deep breaths drinking in the pure air with a hint of minty pine. The pleasant freshness of the tranquil lakes negates the oppressive heat spilling down from the sky.

I walk on in the stillness and silence and my mind wanders to my grandmother. In her youth these lakes weren't part of the national park. She came here to gather water for drinking and household chores. Today swimming in the lakes is strictly forbidden. However, I know of a place where the staff patrolling the area turn a blind eye and let people bathe in the water. I'm headed there now.

The path rounds the corner reaching a small wood beyond where there are some large rocks and another lake into which cascade half a dozen waterfalls. The sound of the tumbling water revives me. I sit on a rock, take off my shoes and dip my toes into the lake. I imagine myself sinking deeper and deeper into an underwater world full of darting fish and the skeletal remains of trees long dead. My separation from the world has gone. I've become one with it, rather than outside looking in. A park warden taps me on the shoulder and startles me. I'm told not to touch the water or risk being fined.

I continue on the path to find a place under the trees with picnic tables and a small restaurant nearby selling simple fare. I close my eyes for a moment to drink from my flask. When I open them I can hear the laugher and shouts of people nearby. Rounding a large oak tree, I see naked bathers, both men and women, splashing and frolicking in the water. I envy their free-spiritedness and unbounded joy.

I sit in the grass nearby and take off my shoes. I notice the piles of clothes of the bathers are rather odd. None of them are modern day garb, but that of a bygone era. Discarded corsets abound, together with britches and caps, white shirts with frilly cuffs and collars. I am jolted by the realisation that what I'm witnessing is from more than a century ago. The span of time has somehow been bridged. My mind has cleaved through the decades. Or, what I see is some kind of mirage, some reflection of a wish to be free and spontaneous again and liberated from the stresses of modern life. The sun is behind a cloud. I take out my apple and eat. I feel so drowsy, the endless possibilities of time's permutations going through my mind. There is some strange force pulling at me to lie down and sleep.

When I wake, it is only a few moments later but the trees are being agitated by a strong breeze, their branches rustling frantically. The bathers are gone now and I ready myself to take the ferry to the other side of the lake, to explore the lower part of the national park. While on the boat I hear from the tourist guide of the legend of the Black Queen. Locals prayed to this woman for help when there was a drought in the area. Her response was to create these lakes. In another of the stories, it is said that a vast amount of treasure lies buried at the bottom of one of the lakes. I muse on this as I step onto shore and another stretch of the path.

The heat is getting a bit oppressive and I feel giddy. Each time I shut my eyes to steady myself I see a vision of the area in the days of drought, peasants thirsting for water. I try not to shut my eyes. I want this vision to disappear. I sit against a tree in the shade fanning myself with my hat. On the lake I see my grandmother standing in a small boat that glides towards me. Beside her is a wolf, and in front of him is a treasure chest, its glittering contents shining in the sun. But as the boat nears shore the vision begins to fade and then dissolve completely.

I hear growling behind me but it's only children playing at being bears, I wonder, morphing into real bears, then morphing into children again. There is nothing to fear, only the heat playing tricks on my mind. But which is the illusory image, the children or the bears, I wonder as I eat a hunk of bread and cheese and feel the strength returning to my body. I continue to the last lake with waterfalls. I crouch and trail my hand in the water and splash some on my face while no one is looking. Someday I want to return here. In the autumn, when my fever is gone, when the Black Queen is not sitting beside me pouring water from an ornate jug into a goblet with treasure lying strewn at my feet. None of the other tourists notice what I see. I pick up one of the coins and examine it. On one side an image of the lakes, and on the other my name. My hand trembles. It's as if dream has merged with reality. I can no longer tell the difference.

I toss the coin into the lake for good luck and notice hundreds of other similar coins there – currency from all over the world. What do I wish for? A long sleep in my old bed at my grandmother's house, she beside me, mopping my brow with a flannel dipped in cold water. I manage to make it back to the main entrance without further incident, though it seems to take a very long time as if I'm walking through treacle. Tommy is waiting by the car, smoking his cigarette, he waves and calls out: "I wait thirty minutes, but no problem. I enjoy birdsong. The lakes did you good. You have colour in cheeks now." I am so relieved to see him that I surprise him with a hug. He's the most real thing I've seen in hours. "No funny business," he says, with a wink and cheeky grin. "Get in car. I drive you home. Lady needs rest. And maybe vodka." I couldn't agree more.

Short Story 3 – Split in Two.

In the summer of 2011 I travelled to Split in Croatia. The rented apartment I'd booked was reached up 72 perspiration-inducing stairs. Inside, the walls were painted with murals by the owner, a boat's skipper who was away all summer steering tourists around the Adriatic islands in his private yacht. Outside was a balmy 35°, perfect for the beach. On my first day there I walked the 200 yards to the promenade that overlooked the bay. I swam for an hour in the briny sway of waves gently caressing and cooling my body. It felt like a great relief after sweltering in my dingy office in London all summer, and the subsequent stay in a claustrophobic Manor House for those receiving treatment for mental health issues.

There weren't many people about now, only a few sunbathers and children playing with beach balls in the shallow part of the sea. I guess there were other parts of Split that were more popular. After my swim I took a detour via the vegetable market to stock up on necessities. I passed a stall selling hand-made wooden items, intricately carved, from chess sets to spinning wheels. This heat was intense and I realised I was overdressed so on the way home I bought a white summer dress from a stall selling good-quality linen products.

The owner, a lady with long white hair and the kind of wrinkles that you see on a prune, handed me some dried lavender with my change. "You need some luck," she said. I haven't a fondness for superstition, but I took the lavender, and thanked her. The next day while walking around the Old Town I had it tucked behind my ear hoping that the aroma would help keep me feeling relaxed. I have spells where I feel quite jittery for no reason. The Doctor said this was to be expected after churning up so many uncomfortable feelings about my past during my stay at the Manor. The white dress fitted perfectly and was cool to the touch. I found the sensation of the soft linen on my skin soothed my nerves.

I walked through a street where a group of singers serenaded a crowd of transfixed onlookers. These were happy romantic songs, but I wasn't feeling in the mood to hear such melodies, so I hurriedly walked on. I saw a gallery where the walls were covered in artworks depicting magical fairy kingdoms, butterflies, princesses, and angels. I liked the colours but the subject matter wasn't to my taste. As a child I would have loved these images but the child in me hadn't been seen for quite some time. Now a certain melancholy pervaded my mind that couldn't resonate with such images and so I walked on, lost in my thoughts.

I was having a break from work as an editor for a magazine. It was a travel magazine I worked for, yet ironically I rarely got the chance to go abroad. It was a high-pressure job, always working to a deadline. I never got enough sleep and always worried if I was doing enough as the editor to keep the readers interested. One of our journalists got seriously ill while in South America and had to be flown home. She needed months of recuperation. Another was arrested on suspicion of being a spy and held in detention for 6 months. Although none of this was my fault, I took full responsibility. The company had to pay legal fees to negotiate to bring our reporter home. The anxiety took its toll on my mind, as did the financial burden.

I was in the Manor for a month trying to get back some equilibrium. While there I was in daily therapy that brought up certain issues from my childhood that had remained buried. My sister had gone missing on a holiday in Croatia when we were eleven and was never found. I had to try and come to terms with this finally. One of the perks of having a nervous breakdown is that you get paid leave until you've recovered. I found the extra cash and the free time were ample encouragement for me to get away from London and to visit the place where my sister was last seen all those years ago. So as soon as I was deemed fit enough to go home, this is what I did.

The story from onlookers goes that my sister Beatrice broke up a crowd of kids on the beach who were using a stick to taunt a small octopus that had washed up on shore. Afraid they were going to harm or kill it, she wrapped the octopus around her arm and walked out to sea. She disappeared from view and was never seen again. The police had to close the case after a year. They assumed she'd drowned while being swept away by a dangerous current. I always refused to believe that story. Beatrice was a good swimmer. She knew about the ways of the sea. And she would never wilfully and knowingly head into danger.

Walking down the cobbled streets of Split's Old Town, I catch my breath as a blonde woman walks by. She's about the age Beatrice would be now. But there are lots of blondes around today so I try not to get distracted. The chances of one actually being my sister are very remote.

I sit outside a restaurant and order a platter of roasted vegetables with rice. Lemonade is on the house, the proper homemade stuff. I eat slowly and thoughtfully, wondering how I will spend my time with the shadow of my sister following me everywhere, making me feel uneasy. There's a sweet family at the next table: the parents and two young girls who look alike and must be sisters. They're giggling about something and a pang of loneliness pierces my heart. I wish I were here with my sister now, not just with an echo of a memory in my mind.

The lavender just then falls out of my hair and onto the table and a blue butterfly alights on it looking for nectar but finding none. Nevertheless it seems very curious about it and stays there while I sip the lemonade. It briefly lands on my ear before flying away. There is a tingle on my skin where it touched me.

A handsome olive-skinned waiter brings the dessert menu. It's here still, Beatrice's favourite pudding, the layered cream cake with pastry that is traditional to this area. It's not my favourite but I will order it anyway. I feel it will bring me in some way closer to my sister to eat what she would have loved to eat. I imagine her sitting opposite me, her ghost envying me with every bite I take. It's silly really, to think like this. As I savour each mouthful of delicately flavoured cream mousse and crispy pastry, memories return of our many holidays here in Croatia before she went missing, of us racing along the beach chasing each other, or sitting in forests of pine playing a miniature game of chess.

She was a keen chess player and wanted to become a grandmaster. We'd practice for a couple of hours and then go for a swim, our parents watching us from the shore. One afternoon, she lost her black queen and accused me of stealing it. She was furious and stormed off angrily. I spent half an hour searching for it amongst the pine needles that littered the forest floor where we'd been sitting, until I found it. She was gazing out to sea in a world of her own and was startled when I tapped her on the shoulder and presented her with the chess piece.

"You shouldn't have hidden it," she said, crossly. "That was cruel."

"If I'd hidden it deliberately, I wouldn't have just spent half an hour searching for it, would I?" came my reply. She screwed up her face, thinking deeply.

"Well, you shouldn't have lost it then," she said.

"I think it wasn't I who lost it, but the fairies of the forest that took it away. They realised it wasn't much use to them as it wasn't edible and so kindly brought it back and left it on the ground for me to find." I could see I was persuading her. She was still such a child. She couldn't hold a grudge against me for long.

"What do you think's out there, at sea?" she asked.

"Mermaids, most definitely mermaids," I told her earnestly.

"Then I'd like to find one," she said.

"I'm sure you will, one day, when the time's right."

It's strange how I remember this conversation. I pay the bill, leaving a generous tip. I'm in a better mood, now that I'm remembering Beatrice again. I stroll to the palm-tree-lined promenade by the marina. The atmosphere is happy and carefree. The sun's rays cover the sky in brilliant ribbons of pink light. But it's all tinged with some sadness that Beatrice can't see this too.

There's a clown on stilts making animals out of balloons for the children in the crowd of onlookers. I go and watch, finding his skilfulness entrancing. He spends some time creating an elaborate fish out of four different balloons. It is so intricate. I gasp when he hands it to me. "For the child within," he says. But the child within me is Beatrice. I imagine her, age 7, receiving the balloon animal, her face lighting up with delight. Inside I feel a warm glow in my heart where before was an empty place filled with sadness.

But just as the grey clouds of sorrow leave my heart, they rapidly fill the sky. We are covered in brooding shadows. The rain comes in a deluge and people scurry for shelter. I huddle with others in an archway that was once part of the old Roman Emperor Diocletian's Palace. Split is awash with ancient history that I've barely been aware of up until now. Imprints of the past mingle with my memories. It's like being in an echo chamber full of moving images. I see Beatrice waving at me before going for a swim, and Emperor Diocletian bestowing on her a medal for bravery. He unveils a sculpture of her, looking heroic, with an octopus wrapped around her arm. What was in that lemonade I had for lunch? I'm feeling decidedly unwell. The rain spell has caused me to feel dizzy. I'm one of those peculiar types whose body and mind are greatly affected by the weather.

The rain abates and I walk, somewhat unsteadily, back through the labyrinth of cobbled streets and past the art gallery again. I do a double take as I notice a new painting in the window of a mermaid with a blue butterfly on her ear. Beside her on the rock is a game of chess, ready to be played. The board and pieces are white and blue, the piercing blue of the sky behind her. Her hand gestures to me as if offering me a match. The mermaid's face is how Beatrice would have looked now. What game is she playing with me? I know she is here somewhere. It can't just be a trick of my mind. The smell of lavender is acute now, though I left the dried flowers behind at the restaurant, and there is nobody around except for me.

What is my next move to be?

I walk into the gallery.

"Welcome," says the owner. "Do please take a look around, and if I can be of help in any way, just let me know."

"The painting in the window, it's new. Who did it?" I ask, trembling.

"Our resident artist. She's in the back of the shop. I'll go get her, if you would like to meet her."

"Please," I say. The owner is gone for a minute or two and then returns with the mermaid's creator. She is not what I expected. She is stooped but young. Her hands are twisted with arthritis. Her eyes twinkle as she greets me. They are the same turquoise colour as her dress and of the sea. I ask her to tell me more about the painting.

"It was a dream I had, of two sisters playing chess," she says. "And then a mermaid took one of them out to sea to become one of the tribe, leaving the other sister behind looking for the missing piece."

"What missing piece?" I ask her.

"The missing child that was within her. The one that vanished the day her sister was swept out to sea, obviously." The artists says this quite crossly, as if it's something I ought to have known.

"The mermaid, she looks like my sister. It's freaking me out. How did you know?" I ask insistently.

"Don't ask *me* why I dream what I dream," the lady says with an air of finality before disappearing into the back annexe once more.

I decide to buy the painting and arrange for it to be shipped to my address in London. I believe the painting isn't some kind of clue as to my sister's whereabouts but a message, from her to me. I'm pretty sure she is telling me that she's okay. She exists in a realm of the imagination and still somehow exerts an influence on this world and on me. There is no death, just traversing from one plane of existence to another. I feel a spark ignite in my chest that sends a warm glow like honey throughout my body, relieving me of dizziness and fatigue. I swiftly reach the open-air market. I know exactly where I'm headed. The guy at the stall I'm looking for is just packing up for the day.

"Please," I say with urgency in my voice. "I'd like the blue and white chess set."

"Good choice," he says. "This one is handmade by my grandfather."

I nod my head, smile appreciatively and hand him double what he is asking.

"Buy your grandfather something nice," I say.

"Vodka," he says, grinning. "Thank you, lady. My lucky day is today."

"Mine too," I say.

Back in the apartment I notice something is different. There's a strong lavender smell and my heart feels a lot lighter than when I arrived a few days ago. I'll be back at work soon in my office in London. I will keep the blue chess set open and displayed on my coffee table at home. Always ready, waiting for Beatrice's next move.

Short Story 4 – Beyond the Summit

In 2008 I stayed at my uncle and aunt's house in a seaside town that is known as the Riviera of Croatia. Located along the Istrian peninsula, it is a gem in the Adriatic suitable for the more well-to-do tourist. The apartment, reached by a quantity of steps ascending to it, was perched on the hill with great views overlooking the bay and nearby tennis courts. Down on the promenade were a number of boutique shops that only those with a generous budget could afford. Luckily a health shop and grocers stocked adequate amounts of vegetarian food. The only things worth eating out for were the ice-creams at The Grand Hotel.

On my third visit there the waiter recognised me and offered to show me the main ballroom. The high ceilings and faded grandeur with red velvet curtains, flocked wallpaper and a central magnificent chandelier looked to be from a pre-First World War era. No longer functioning as a ballroom, this was the dining room for the hotel's many guests. Now, out of season, it was quiet. The light coming through the large windows illuminated the dust in the air. It was like something from a giant cruise liner, the Titanic, perhaps.

I chose to sit outside by the swimming pool and watch a solitary diver practice his elaborate somersaults from the high board. Eventually, finding the allure of the Hotel just as faded as its interiors, I decided to take a bus to a nearby seaside village where the prospect of finding a good beach was much better. On my arrival, I was lucky enough to find a tourist office. I was encouraged by the young lady inside to visit the waterfall, reached by a bus that left the station every two hours. She said it was an experience I shouldn't miss. The next bus was due in five minutes. I had no time to think. I decided to take the ride up the hill and see what I could see. Swimming would have to wait.

The vehicle in question looked like a 1960's American school bus. As I stepped inside I was reminded of the Beatles song 'The Magical Mystery Tour'. I wondered what lay ahead and hoped it was worth the detour from my carefully laid plans. A few other people got on before the driver, a portly, sweaty gentleman in a white uniform, took his seat. The engine revved. And then we were off. The pace was slow at first as we turned large bend after bend in the hillside. Gradually it got steeper, the bends sharper, and the speed faster.

The bus was lurching all over the place as we appeared to be ascending a spiralling road that was barely wide enough to let the oncoming traffic pass by. As we went higher, the precipitous drop into the valley below looked more and more treacherous. But the driver and other passengers seemed oblivious to the danger. I tried to grab the bar in front of my seat but my palms were sweating so much that I could hardly hold on. At times – all too frequent times in my opinion – the wheels came dangerously close to going over the side of the road and into the sheer drop that, had we tumbled over, would have smashed the bus and its passengers into countless pieces.

I prayed like I had never prayed before. This was quite a lengthy process, being, as I was, a Unitarian. I prayed that our driver knew what he was doing. And then... we were airborne. We'd reached the summit of the hill and travelled beyond it. Out of the window I could see the valley below growing ever smaller. The spiral road around the hill was no more than a distant form, covered in mist. Cars appeared like matchboxes and large trees no more significant than tiny shrubs.

My stomach lurched. I wasn't good with heights. In my current state of anxious confusion I was now convinced that my prayers had been answered and a miracle had occurred. It was only when there was little reaction from the driver and passengers that I realised that either this happened all the time or I was dreaming. I remembered a short story I'd read some years previously called *The Celestial Omnibus* by E.M. Forster. Could this be what he was talking about?

Clouds were around us now and the temperature was so cool that I was shivering.

"No parking at the top," said the driver. "I have to circle until a space is available. Happens all the time. No need to worry. Only, petrol is running low."

At this point I stopped praying and put my despairing head in my hands. Still, it brought no comfort. Some of the other passengers were complaining, saying that they hadn't got all day to visit their aunt/ sister/ friend.

"Tourist spot," said the driver pointing below to the summit of the hill. "Very popular." He articulated each syllable as if explaining the situation to a child. The engine stuttered then spluttered and then it completely conked out. My heart shot into my mouth as we went into free-fall, spinning downwards, out of control, as was my fear.

"No need to worry, folks," said the driver, calmly. I seriously wondered why not. Was this the most blindly optimistic person in the universe? It turned out the driver had come prepared. Reaching into a small compartment on the dashboard he turned a knob and pressed a button. I felt the bus shudder as if something had jerked it upwards. Someone leaned out of the window and looked up before informing us that a giant parachute had opened up above us, guiding us gently back downward as if the bus weighed nothing at all.

We eventually landed with a bump and a wobble on another vehicle at the hill's highest point. They really must do something about the parking round here, I thought. The doors sprung open and with another prod of a button, some steps unfolded to lead us finally onto terra firma once again. That's when the world stopped shaking but for some reason I seemed to continue with this involuntary motion. A passenger turned to me and could see my shocked expression.

"You're obviously a tourist. Locals know the deal around here," she said. "See, you were worried for nothing," she said dismissively, as if I was some weakling from abroad who needed to toughen up and start trusting the universe more.

"Where can I get a drink around here?" I asked her. She chuckled and pointed to the guesthouse down the road. I headed there with all the speed I could muster, clasping my sunhat to my head, and wobbling on the pebbles as if I'd already had a few too many drinks to mention. Sitting outside on the patio of the lodge, I took long deep breaths to steady my nerves and when the waiter arrived I tried to feign the semblance of a smile. But it wasn't convincing at all.

"Tough journey?" he enquired with a wink.

"Tough enough," I said.

"Will that be the drinks menu you require, Madam?" he said, smiling.

"Dessert menu too, please." I rubbed my arm where I had bruised it against the window.

"It was that bad, huh?"

"The journey could've been a little smoother," I replied. It was the understatement of the year.

"Menu coming right up," he said before disappearing into the gloomy interior of the lodge. "Sit tight. I won't be a minute."

It wasn't as if I was going anywhere anyway. My legs had other plans. They wanted me to sit right here for as long as it took until they stopped shaking.

I ordered a slice of raspberry cheesecake and a glass of brandy. I'd heard brandy was good for shock. When it arrived it did not hang about for long. And I didn't want to either. That waiter seemed to take some kind of pleasure in my suffering and when he handed me the bill, I knew why. I guess being the only eatery between here and the moon allowed them to charge anything they liked. And they certainly did. With the obligatory tip, I hadn't enough money for the return fare. If I'd bought a return ticket at the outset, I'd be doing the washing up now to pay for my bill. I counted my lucky stars I hadn't. I hated cleaning crockery, with a passion.

My brandy-infused legs managed to get me off the patio and follow the signs to the waterfall. I had to pass some workmen on the way. What were they fixing? I wondered. Everything around here operated so efficiently. They were digging a hole in the road. Perhaps trying to get from this God-forsaken place to Australia. I didn't blame them. But when I called out an emphatic "I don't blame you!" at them as I passed, they just looked bemused. Realising my mistake I asked them where the waterfall was and they indicated with wild gesticulations. I carried on walking.

Soon I could hear the sound of the waterfall. A lilting lovely cascade of watery melodies drew me closer and closer. And there it was, the tiniest waterfall I had ever seen. Surely this couldn't be it, the legendary falls that I had come all this way to see. But yes it was. I sat down on a rock and wept. I wept for my shaky legs, for not being tough enough and for the 'raspberry cheesecake surprise' at the lodge that was bereft of raspberries. Perhaps that was the surprise. I also wept because I knew I would have to walk back on foot but then the sad tears turned into tears of relief because I at least didn't have to get on that damn bus again. I took a sip from my canteen and headed back into the fray. The workmen were having their lunch.

"Great waterfall, no?" asked one of them.

"Just perfect," I said, forcing a smile.

"Lucky waterfall," said another, with a mouthful of salami and cheese.

"Lucky indeed," I said as I wended my way passed them and onto the main road.

"Walking? Go that way," said the third, pointing to an overgrown path between rows of houses that descended into the valley. It didn't look so bad. How hard could this be? In fact, I could do it barefoot and would now have to as the strap on one of my sandals had broken.

The slow amble downhill was pleasant, and gradually I relaxed. Either side of me were back gardens that were mostly used as allotments. And beyond those were quaint cottages like something out of a fairy tale. The cool earth beneath my feet was very grounding. Soon the bus, the road, and the waterfall were all distant memories to me. I was soothed by the stillness, healed of my ordeal by the birdsong, butterflies, and bees. I stopped by a gate and drank in all the scents and sounds. Lavender, rose, and sage filled the air with their aromas.

A couple of squirrels chasing each other scurried past. One stopped nearby to look at me, assessing if I was likely to have any morsels of food to give her. I reached into my bag and found a couple of old crackers from a previous day's hike. I crumbled them and tossed them in her direction. Not interested in what I had to offer, she scampered off. It was a plump robin that hungrily devoured the offerings. I whistled a tune and it whistled back. Our call and refrain went on for a few minutes until it flew off into a garden full of ripe tomatoes and grapes on the vine. I was tempted to pick a few but thought that might steal away the magic of the moment. Remembering the fate that befell Peter Rabbit, I walked on glad of the opportunity to enjoy this quiet interlude from the glamorous artifice of the seaside promenade with its classy hotels and chic shops in such a picturesque place as this. This is what I'd come on this holiday for. I wasn't here to acquire a tan and a lot of silly souvenirs. I'd come to escape from the everyday business of life and from my busy mind.

Then I saw it, a vision in the bushes that was the ultimate souvenir of my trip: a deer mother and its fawn. They gazed at me as if bestowing on me some kind of blessing from some ancient time and place with wisdom now lost to humankind. They seemed surrounded by a golden aura of light that made their silky coats shine and their eyes glisten. I looked into the eyes of this deer and felt its fragile gentle soul. I felt honoured it had taken the time to acknowledge me and show no fear. Then the image of the animals dissolved and I was left with a golden glow inside.

I started to hum a tune and I felt transported to a time long ago, before the age of the dusty ballroom and the crazy vehicles that clog our cities. I felt at one with nature, part of it, and not an outsider looking in. But the path came to an end, and I had to enter civilization once more. I found a bank near the tourist office and withdrew some euros. I would buy some lunch and then walk to the beach that I was told was nearby. I asked the lady at the tourist office if I could expect anything out of the ordinary again, and she looked at me like I was mad. Buses parachuting out of the sky must be part of the norm around here.

After dining at a nearby restaurant without any unusual incidents, there was a sudden downpour. I sheltered under some trees, enjoying the aroma of the wet earth and minty scent of the pine needles, while thunder and lightning tore across the sky. It was not safe to be there under such dramatic conditions. I decided to head home to the house by the sea. I'd had enough excitement for now. When I arrived back in town, the sky was as clear and as blue as the ocean. The storm had passed and so had my anger and dissatisfaction. I had no need to go hunting after magnificent waterfalls or eat cheesecake with raspberries. These fleeting pleasures of the senses were pale experiences compared to feeling at one with the world.

Back home in London I sit in my garden, now filled with herbs and flowers from the Adriatic regions. The scents of lavender and rosemary take me back to that special place in Croatia many years ago. There are so many butterflies and bees enjoying it here too. I sip my mint tea from herbs grown here. And today, as every day since my return, a mother deer and its faun visit me, bathed in a golden light. I have created a sculpture of them that's on display in a gallery. It's made of layers of coloured glass and lit from within by a golden light. Since retirement, evening classes have become sacred to me. I am forever creating deer in any material I can find, from twigs and dried flowers to copper wire and wool. I've become known as 'the deer lady'. Any money I make gets put back into the garden with all the plants I buy.

Mother and faun are doing well. They never change or grow old. While I, now in retirement, with ailing health, can no longer travel abroad. But here is my sanctuary. I know the time will come when I will have to leave this place and my beloved visitors behind, my angels in animal form. Before then I will dedicate this area as a peace garden and welcome people in. Perhaps I will return to visit one day as a squirrel or bird and enjoy being here again. Only time will tell what nature and the mysterious realms of existence have in store for me at the end of my allotted time here on earth.

Short Story 5 – Taking a Step Back

Baska, Island Krk, Croatia, 2007

Today I took the bus from the small apartment where I'm staying in the old town of Krk to a popular seaside resort called Baska. The bus journey was a little arduous in the heat and with all the twists and turns on the road I was feeling a little travel sick. On my arrival, I enquired as to the location of the local shops and found a small pub in which to get a soft drink to settle my stomach. It was gloomy inside and like something out of a Dickens novel. Beer was served from wooden barrels that looked like they'd been around since the 17th century. The whole place had the musty air of a pirates' hangout. I was expecting to see some crusty old sea-captain with an eye-patch walk out of the lavatory brandishing a pistol. Instead there was a young woman at the bar who became quite concerned when I told her I was feeling unwell. In addition to my soft drink she made me some ginger tea according to her mother's recipe for nausea. Both beverages were gratefully received.

After a while the room stopped spinning and my legs felt a lot more solid. Then a well-dressed couple entered the otherwise empty pub. This man and woman were arguing about the finer points of levitation. They seemed oblivious to their surroundings they were so involved in their heated conversation. I was intrigued by the subject matter because the art of levitation had always fascinated me, ever since I read the autobiography of Nikola Tesla who claimed to have had that rare ability. The woman was insistent that she had seen someone levitating in the market area just a moment ago but the man asserted that she had been tired and her mind was inventing things. It was fortunate that I had exceptional hearing, because although they were sat in a corner by the window speaking quietly, I could hear every word.

"You mustn't talk to anyone about your strange visions, Clarice," said the man.

"These weren't visions. You're so closed-minded," she said.

"Wasn't it I who dutifully came to all of those Buddhist classes with you for months on end? I don't call that closed-minded," he argued.

"John, it was obvious you were just there to smugly dismiss all that was being said and to indulge in the free food after the talks."

"Well, I'm particularly fond of Vietnamese cooking. And really, darling, reincarnation is such a ridiculous concept." John swatted a fly that had landed on his arm. Clarice winced and had a sharp intake of breath.

"You need to clear your karma before you die, honey, or there's no knowing what you'll become in your next life." Clarice looked very concerned. I hid behind a menu I was holding in order not to look too conspicuous.

"Reincarnation, levitation – it's all the same kind of nonsense," said John. "Remember when you were into dream-catchers to prevent your nightmares and tree-hugging to improve your energy field? Did that amount to anything?"

"Why does everything have to amount to something tangible? There are unseen worlds where mysterious things happen. I'm just trying to tune in." Clarice picked up a napkin that had been laid on the table and dabbed her forehead with it. It was very stuffy in here, with little ventilation. The heat felt oppressive.

"I'm sorry life is so unbearably dull with me that you need to escape into all this mystical nonsense," John said grumpily.

"I do wonder," said Clarice thoughtfully, "If there isn't some major blockage in your aura. Too much blue and grey and not enough red and yellow."

"Really? Can we give this subject a rest and order us a nice vegan lunch instead? I could eat a horse I'm so hungry!"

"Horses aren't exactly a vegan item, John, dear. Do you never stop thinking about your stomach?"

What an odd pair, but I guess opposites attract. I felt a strange tingle down my spine that I usually feel when something happens that I know is part of my destiny. John would have probably called this idea hogwash but Clarice would have been on my side. I knew I was meant to hear this conversation. I had to go and find the levitating being in the marketplace. But first I needed to use the restroom.

Inside was not what I'd expected. The door itself was like a saloon door out of the Wild West. It swung back and forth and had no lock on it for some reason. This worried me a little but I got on with what I needed to do. The toilet was old fashioned and the tap fittings too, made of brass, added to the air of times gone by. I was absorbed by my reflection in the mirror; the laughter lines around my eyes and my greying hair, unruly as ever. I remembered my youth, going to comedy clubs and Jazz nights in town after days at university. I temporarily lost track of time.

When I stepped back into the bar, it was unrecognisable. The fixtures and fittings were the same but the atmosphere was thick with smoke and the raucous conversation of many people gathered at the different tables. When the smoke cleared a bit I could see they were in 18th century garb. Was this some kind of costume party? Some instinct deep inside told me it wasn't. Clarice and John and the barmaid were gone. Instead were a group of sailors singing shanties, and another group engaging in a card game for cash with 18th Century playing cards and money. A plump and buxom barmaid was cajoling the customers to order her meat pies. My day job is to work for a women's magazine specialising in true-life mysteries and psychic phenomena. It was just a job. I wasn't a believer. But this turned things on its head.

Nobody noticed me as I milled about the room, overhearing snippets of conversation. The journalist in me was intrigued. People often wrote in to tell me of their experiences going through magical portals into other realms. That used to make me scoff in disbelief. Now I wasn't so sure. One man slapped the serving girl on the rump and she slapped him hard on the face. Another piratical-looking gent spat on the floor and hammered the table with his cutlery, demanding to be served.

"Tell us about your cargo from the East, Marko," said one man to another, sat at the table by the window. A fly buzzed angrily against the glass hopelessly, trying to get out.

"Exotic animals and spices," was Marko's reply. "We have a tiger on board. Ferocious creature. The Indian farmers were only too glad to be rid of her."

"What does a tiger look like? I've never seen one, only heard of them," said the first man.

"Biggest looking fangs you'll ever see, and a growl as loud as thunder. Long whiskers like Zoran over there and a coat of white, orange and black fur. Claws like knives. Not to be messed with, Niko." Marko took a long drag of his cigar, exhaled slowly creating smoke rings in the air, and bit into his steaming meat pie. Niko looked pale and troubled.

"Don't worry yourself, young fellow," said Marko, meat juices dripping down his chin. "She isn't going nowhere but to a wealthy Venetian merchant in Rijeka. She may be a man-eater but we'd shoot her dead soon as she'd escape if ever she did so. And she's clapped in irons strong enough to hold a beast of the strength of ten men."

I wandered back to my table and sat down. I shut my eyes and prayed this strange vision would go away. When I opened them again, the room was back to how it was before. Clarice and John were eating a vegan lunch in the corner, in silence. The bargirl was drying glasses with a cloth. I paid the bill and went on my way, so relieved that things were appearing ordinary once again.

I decided to amble along the pedestrian street of quaint shops that were nearby. Each one was made in a rough way with uneven doors and windows and sloping roofs. The exteriors of the buildings were plastered in white that reflected the sun's bright dazzle. I was attracted to one shop in particular that sold gifts and trinkets. Outside was hanging a tapestry with an embroidered tiger on the front. A written inscription on it read, "It is better to live one day as a tiger, than 1000 years as a sheep." This quote was stated to be a Tibetan proverb. How odd to encounter another tiger reference in so short a space of time.

Stepping into the shop to take a look around, I wondered what it would be like to live as a tiger for one day. Surely I would want to eat all the sheep that were living for 1,000 years. I did once have an inkling of what it was like to be a tiger when I quit my job of 13 years because of a disagreement with the boss. He'd given a newly employed worker with less experience than me a promotion to the position in the company that I should have inherited in my journey up the career ladder. Feeling underappreciated and snubbed after all my efforts at work I decided to make a fresh start as a writer. That is how I ended up penning articles for women's magazines. I wasn't exactly happy there, but it paid the bills and provided some holiday money too, which made up for the ludicrous stuff I sometimes had to write.

Recently I interviewed a woman who believed that her cat had psychic powers and she cited many examples of this special kitty's abilities. Although I'm a bit of a cynic I must admit it all sounded very believable and the story I wrote based on the interview was promoted on the front page. People so love cats that this edition outsold all our others. Unfortunately there are only so many stories about cats to write about, so I came to Baska on my well-earned break after three years of writing published articles, to soak up a bit of the atmosphere and the sunshine and to begin to write my first novel. I could do with the extra income, and the diversion, after the disappointment of a promising relationship that had ended badly.

I thought of writing something light-hearted, set during one summer abroad. There would be an Englishwoman with a sheltered upbringing who was quite reserved, discovering the joys of living a more free-spirited life. Additional subplots would include rescuing some children from an evil gypsy, romance involving a handsome sea-captain with a parrot, and foiling a plot to kidnap a wealthy but stupid millionaire. My heroine would receive ample reward, and a day's outing on a luxury yacht that would capsize in choppy waters, requiring said heroine to single-handedly rescue all of the crew. At some point in the story I wanted to introduce a psychic cat as I thought the addition of such an animal would surely boost sales of my novel. Perhaps a cat was too tame an addition and a tiger would add more drama. I was wondering if the inclusion of a talking animal would be plausible in such a book when I felt a little faint and decided to leave the shop.

I was feeling quite lightheaded as I went in search of the market, for it was the levitating person I wanted to see. It must have been the excitement of having an unexpected lead to follow that was making me feel this way. It couldn't be far, and I would enjoy exploring the area until I discovered the place in question.

I walked through the winding streets. There were no cars, only people, some on bicycles and some on foot. The pavement seemed to slope this way and that in an uneven fashion and the construction of the buildings either side looked like sloppily created cakes melting in the heat. Here and there were hanging baskets full of colourful arrays of blooms. The vivid mauves and pinks vibrated with colour and energy. The blue of the sky was incredibly intense and seemed saturated with this particular blueness providing a canopy above. Despite the beauty around me, I was feeling lost and a bit confused. All of the streets looked much the same. The gulls were circling so I knew I was very near the coast. I was sweating now and longed for a swim but which way to turn to extricate myself from the labyrinth, I did not know. Then I saw it and I froze.

About 20 yards away was a tiger. It faced me and stared right into my eyes. I wondered if the heat was affecting me in some way. I reached out for a wall to steady myself and luckily that was as real as anything else around me. I took some deep breaths and the tiger walked towards me. I wondered if I was dreaming. Had I fallen asleep on the bus and was I still asleep? Had I even really arrived at Baska in the first place? And were Clarice and John merely figments of my vivid imagination? And what about the pub with people from 300 years ago? Or was this all really happening and this the very tiger the man Marko had spoken of, transported through some portal in time? I thought I'd take a chance in this strange new world unfolding before me and talk to the tiger.

"What is it that you want?" I asked, trembling. Nobody else was about; it was just us two facing each other. But for some reason the tiger didn't feel like a stranger to me but someone I knew very well.

"This isn't about what *I* want," the tiger said. "It's all about what *you* are after."

"And what do you think that is?" I queried.

"It is what you've always been looking for," replied the creature. Then it snarled and I took a step back, tripping on a wonky paving slab and falling, twisting my ankle.

"You should watch where you're going!' said the tiger angrily. Then its mood shifted. "Sometimes, however, you need to take a step back in order to move forwards."

"But I don't know where I'm going, or what it is that I ultimately seek," I said.

"Remember, what you are looking for will never be found because you are looking in the wrong place." The tiger smiled knowingly. But I was smarting. It felt like a smack in the face to be reprimanded by this magnificent beast. The pain in my ankle was intense. It was quickly swelling up and a bruise was appearing. I tried to think what it was that I was looking for that this tiger knew all about.

"Don't think too hard," said she. "It's staring you in the face." I looked to my left in order to lean on a lamppost to get up off the ground and as I did so I saw my reflection in a window. It startled me for a moment because I thought in that instant, who is this woman staring back at me with such a compassionate-looking face and such sweet wise eyes. I was surprised that it was in fact me. If I am such a compassionate person, then why am I so angry that I have tripped and fallen, and made to look a fool by a tiger that may or may not be imaginary, and completely lost my way.

The Tiger turned to leave.

"Oh no!" I cried, "You mustn't leave yet. We were just getting to know one another."

The tiger turned its head and it looked very sad. Was it sad to be leaving, perhaps?

"The person you're looking for is yourself, and the thing you want is within you," said the creature, before slowly walking away around the end of the street. When I hobbled to that corner and looked around there was no sign of her. If my mind was playing tricks on me, I was sure there was some meaning behind it, some missing puzzle piece I was meant to discover. I was being shown some clues to my own self's workings. Here, at last, was my chance to discover something momentous that could change my life forever.

Short Story 6 – An Unusual Elevation

My ankle was throbbing painfully and I needed to find somewhere to sit down and take stock. I was now in a different street from all the others. The buildings here looked more defined and less slapdash. The paving was even and didn't make me feel giddy walking along it. I came across a shop selling an assortment of umbrellas; I bought a black-and-white one to use as a walking stick and keep the weight off my ankle. Then I found a cafe and ordered a sandwich. I looked at my watch. It was late afternoon. Where had all the time gone? I hadn't been walking for that long.

The sandwich was dry and pretty tasteless but I was eager for something to fill my stomach other than the jangle of nerves I was feeling, and so I ate it hungrily. The bus back to the old town didn't leave until 5.30 so I still had time to find the market. This time I asked directions and was told it was just around the corner. When I went inside the cafe to pay my bill I saw an enormous mural on the far side of the wall depicting a tiger in a forest. I could have sworn in that moment that the painted animal winked at me. I pretended not to have noticed.

Around the corner the stallholders at the market were packing up for the day. Only an old lady in a black headscarf, knitted dress, and white apron, stayed on. Her delicious-looking produce was on display on a table balanced on some wine crates. She greeted me warmly and told me it was all home–grown in her back garden and watered by a clear steam nearby. For some reason she wanted me to buy the oranges most of all. She said I could try one and cut it open with a knife. She offered me a slice and I didn't want to refuse and so I sucked on the pulp and let the juice run down my chin. I gave her a smile and a thumbs-up. She put the rest of the oranges in a bag and gave them to me.

"Take the juice of one orange, half a glass of milk and one raw egg. Mix and drink. You will feel as strong as a tiger," she said. I thanked her for her advice and got out my purse to pay for the oranges but she refused payment. I was slightly regretting accepting her gift as the added weight caused more pain to surge through my ankle, causing me to wince despite propping myself on the umbrella as I walked.

"If only you could fly," she said, chuckling.

"I wish," I said, resting the bag of oranges on a wall for a moment. Then one by one, each orange rose out of the bag and into the air. I gasped but the old woman just continued to chuckle. Her eyes were now moist with laughter. Was she a witch that had cast a spell? I tried to grab the oranges but they were out of reach, to my great relief, because now I wouldn't have to take them home with me. Then the pain in my ankle disappeared. And I felt as if I was floating on air. I looked down and my feet were several inches off the ground. I really was floating on air. As the day had unfolded I felt less and less surprised by the strange things that were happening. Now I was just happy that the pain was gone. A small child with a balloon pointed up at me but his mother was preoccupied with their dog and she ignored him. Then I saw Clarice staring at me, mouth agape. John was beside her but it was obvious to me he could see nothing. I had the odd feeling that time had folded back in on itself and I was the levitating person that I had overheard Clarice and John discuss in the pub all those hours ago.

The old woman smiled at me.

"You have your wish," she said. "You are flying now."

"But how do I get down again?" I asked her.

"Don't worry about the future, enjoy yourself while you can," she said, and began to pack up the fruit and vegetables on her stall. I was ascending higher and higher until I was level with the top of the lamppost where a gull stood watchfully, on guard. I could see the bay and all the swimmers in the sea, the rocks and sunbathers, and the people in restaurants enjoying their food. I could see Clarice and John in the distance arguing. If wishes really do come true then this was a fine time to have one happen. I wondered what more I could manifest just with the power of my own thoughts. So, with the force of my intention I travelled, airborne, towards the sea. I wasn't sure how long my flying ability was going to last. I had to make the most of it and go exploring.

I flew over the restaurants, smelling the delicious aromas of food wafting up to me and also inhaled the smoke of the grilled meat pervading the air. Then, just before the rocks were gardens of tropical flowers whose colours and scents were particularly intense. Over the rocks and bathers on beach towels and out to sea, I felt exhilarated and light. The warm air caressed my face as I flew by. Looking down at the sea itself, the azure blue and turquoise green was a thing of great beauty to me. I dived into the water and rose up again into the air, sky and clouds above me. I felt like a dolphin, enjoying somersaults just for the fun of it.

The beach was distant now and I could see a fleet of ships on the horizon. They were not the luxury ocean liners common to this area but 18th century vessels. The wooden frames with cannons poised, and the huge sails of the ships were majestic. One of these must have been the cargo of animals and spices. I saw it then, the huge cage on board deck, and the tiger within, curled up and looking defeated, in chains. How could she be in two places at once? It was definitely her I had seen in the streets of Baska. Had she special powers? She saw me and rose to her feet. She was limping like I had been, her ankle twisted and swollen. Yet some part of her being was elsewhere, I could tell, for her eyes were distant and she was not the self-possessed creature I had previously encountered. I could tell this creature on board ship was near death, her face a picture of grief as the strength ebbed slowly from her body. The infection in her foot must have spread. There was nothing I could do.

I was not visible to any of the crew and so I flew onto the deck and put my hand through the cage, touching her head. She lay down and purred as I stroked her chin and then she was gone, now just a lifeless and empty body.

"She's dead!" shouted Marko, angrily. "You were supposed to be looking after her. What will we tell the merchant in Rijeka now?" he addressed the man who had been on vigil, caring for the tiger.

"He has a nice rug now. Safer this way," replied the seaman. Marko knocked the man off his feet with a brutal punch and I felt like cheering. Tigers were not born to become fluffy decorations for the rooms of the wealthy and ignorant with their cold, unfeeling hearts.

Saddened by this turn of events, I decided to return to shore. I could feel my energy waning but as I passed by the familiar rocks I looked up and could see my tiger on a distant hill surveying it all, strong and majestic and proud. She looked completely contented now in this elevated position that I too was sharing. I felt we had a kinship that would remain although we might in future be miles apart.

I made it to the bus stop just in time to board the vehicle waiting there, engine idling. No one seemed to question why I was levitating inside of it and why I couldn't fasten my seatbelt. Nobody here was like John who disbelieved in all things mysterious.

On arriving in the old town once more, I hovered back to the apartment, where I finally reached terra firma again. Luckily there was ice in the freezer in a big plastic bag and it went straight on my ankle. I must have fallen asleep because when I woke the swelling and the bruise was gone, completely. The ice had melted, and, it seemed, so had my troubled heart. I no longer felt angry at all the things I'd been unable to accomplish in life; the perfect job, the perfect relationship, and the greatly admired debut novel. All of that didn't seem to matter now.

I was going to have one hell of a story to tell in my magazine of psychic and mystical phenomena. Whether I was to be believed or not or if I was ever able to levitate again, I knew in my mind what I was really capable of and that gave me a huge sense of peace. When I found that peace,

I realised what the tiger had said was true, all I was really looking for was myself, just a more peaceful version. If there was any treasure to be found, it was already inside me and always had been. No pirate could ever steal it. And like a diamond it would never tarnish. I realised this must be the same for everyone else too. I returned from the holiday with no fear of the future and a sense that the mysterious workings of the universe were going in my favour, in all our favours, ultimately. It seemed I had found some kind of portal into another realm, and into my own heart. Who knew where this might take me in the future, but it felt full of promise.

From that day forward I drank the old woman's special concoction every day and indeed I felt my strength increasing greatly. I wasn't going to live every day as a sheep anymore. When I looked in the mirror now, it was tiger's eyes that looked back at me, full of magic and power. Somewhere deep inside, that tiger and I were now one. Fearless and bold, all I needed now was to find the wisdom to take the next step, forwards this time and not back.

Short Story 7 – A Wall Between Us

Dubrovnik, Croatia, 2004

The coach arrived at the hotel after dark. I was the only one around and was offered a cold supper in the dining room. From what I could tell, the place was very stately. But only daylight would reveal the building's true majesty. Not long after dining, I was shown to my room. It was simple and comfortable with a red carpet and red bed linen. There were green shutters on the window and a small TV. I slept well after my day of travelling and noticed nothing at all peculiar about my surroundings.

At breakfast, which was served on embroidered linen tablecloths, I ordered scrambled eggs and toast, and freshly ground coffee. There were quite a few people in the vast dining room, sedately eating and talking quietly. Most were couples or families, but at the next table to me was an elderly woman who caught my attention. She had long white hair tied up at the sides and piled on top of her head in an old-fashioned and regal style. Her skin was dark brown from the sun and wrinkled like a prune. Her light, bright summer dress was accentuated by a string of pearls around her neck. She had the elegant and graceful demeanour of a dancer. When she looked up at me, her eyes were a clear pale blue. They sparkled with intelligence. I hoped I would get to know this lady that had an air of Miss Marple about her, for she and I were both alone in a sea of people who were not.

I wondered where she'd be spending the day, and when I encountered her in the lift on the way back to my room, I asked her.

"I'm going nowhere but the side of the hotel pool today," came her reply. Her English accent was upper class, and her manner a little imperious as would befit someone of royal status.

"Don't the Old Town or the beaches tempt you in any way?" I asked, wondering what was so alluring about staying in the hotel grounds.

"At my age, which is 96, by the way, trekking around isn't for me. I have only one excursion booked on a boat to one of the islands and that's it. This aged body has seen better days. I've been coming to this hotel for the last 30 years. Back then I could climb to the top of Dubrovnik's old roman wall. I couldn't make it up two steps today."

I felt sorry for her deteriorated health that came with her advanced years. But she was still taking holidays, on her own as well, and that was something.

"Perhaps I'll see you around the pool one afternoon," I said.

"Whatever you wish," she said. "I'm there most of the day except during mealtimes. Having some company would make a change. Nobody bothers to talk to someone my age. They must think I'm completely senile by now."

She said all this matter-of-factly and without any self-pity. I told her I was sure that wasn't the case and that people were just too preoccupied with their companions to make conversations with strangers. She looked surprised, as if my reassuring words were the oddest thing she had ever heard. She'd obviously got used to being ignored. How sad, I thought. The lift arrived at my floor and we said our farewells. She gave me a little wave of her hand and I noticed her perfectly manicured red fingernails. They glistened like rubies.

I took the coach to the Old Town. There was a small bridge and ancient gate to reach the interior of the walled town. Many tourists milled about, although it was late September and the end of the tourist season. The beige paving of the long pedestrian 'road' looked like marble and the stonework of the buildings here were tinted pink by the sun. A man selling gelato was in demand and kids played football around a fountain that looked to be from renaissance times. I walked the length of the shops selling anything from souvenirs to shoes and turned a corner into a square where the cathedral stood. The architecture was beautiful, being particularly ornate around the main entrance. I wanted to go inside but a wedding was taking place so I sat at a nearby cafe and ordered an espresso.

It was mighty hot and by the time my drink arrived, the married couple emerged from that fine edifice in a shower of confetti. The bride looked familiar; she had the same clear light blue eyes as my Miss Marple and I was taken aback at how her smile also curled up in the corner just like my elderly hotel companion's had. She wore a pearl necklace and her dress was satin and lace in the style of 1930's fashion. Her husband also looked from this epoch, with slicked-back hair and a monocle on his left eye. He walked with a cane and looked very dapper. He must have been 25 or so years older than the bride. The pageboys and bridesmaids also wore the elegant clothes of this bygone era. I wondered if this was a 'themed' wedding. The bride and groom danced down the steps as if they were ballet dancers and the assembled crowd cheered.

The sight of this joyous event lifted my spirits but then it started to rain; gently at first and then a deluge as the heavens opened. I was fortunate as the café awnings were shielding me, but the wedding party was drenched, despite the groom covering the bride's shoulders in his coat. Her hair that had been piled elegantly atop her head with ringlets cascading down the sides was now bedraggled and frizzy. Her mascara ran down her face and her wet veil clung to her back and arms like a spider's web. The couple ran into the café, she sobbing, the tears being indistinguishable from the rain on her cheeks, and he reassuring her with comforting words. I felt sorry for them both to have encountered this late September downpour.

She slumped into a chair and he ordered some brandy. Her crying lessened as the rain clouds cleared. He used his handkerchief to wipe the mascara and tears from her face and she brightened up a lot after his tender attentions and her restorative drink. After paying the bill they went on their way. The rest of the wedding party had taken refuge from the rain under some scaffolding to the east side of the building, where it was having some restoration work done. Now they emerged to console the bride and groom. Soon the tears turned to laughter and they all walked off, I presumed to the wedding reception. There might be music and dancing until late in the evening: 1930's music, no doubt.

I walked to the edge of the marina where small boats were moored to take people on excursions. One poster promised a day of island hopping and lunch. I would do that tomorrow. Today I wanted to tackle the famous wall. It surrounds the Old Town and was created to keep out pirates and other possible invaders. It was considered a symbol of liberty. Built in the 12th century and then also in the 17th, after an earthquake in 1667, it is one of the main landmarks here. Now a protected UNESCO heritage site, I was alarmed to see some bullet holes in the side of it at ground level as a result of the recent homeland war.

But today was peaceful, the only unrest a toddler who was screaming for more ice-cream. I paid my ticket and began to ascend the stone steps. Being medieval, they were uneven and narrow. By the time I reached the top I was out of breath and had to sit down. The wall is wide and therefore serves as a walkway around the city, dotted with fortresses that would have been vantage points and armed defence positions when they were in use.

I took in the view; the red-roofed terracotta houses tiered on a slope across the town looked very picturesque. This would be a great setting for a movie, I thought. Beyond them was the bay with a long beach full of bathers reclining under some palm trees. It may have been September but it was still very hot and the promise of a dip in the crystal-clear blue sea was greatly inviting. After eating the apple I'd brought from breakfast, I was refreshed enough to stroll along part of the wall.

My vertigo didn't do me any favours and at several points I felt dizziness rising within. Being a firm believer in mind-over-matter, I tried to master the feelings of nausea and shaky legs. One doctor had suggested I actually face my fear and try seeing what I was like at a certain height. He'd given me a hypnotherapy CD that he was convinced would work. I tried to imagine that I had wings and that there was no need to fear falling. When that didn't work, I visualized strong roots growing from my feet deep into the earth, grounding me. This was a little better. I'm sure a swig of brandy might have steadied my nerves even more, but alas all I had on me was water.

A woman could see I was struggling and asked how I was. My laboured breathing must have given it away. But I was taught to breathe deeply to reduce the anxiety. I thanked her for her concern but said I'd be okay. She wasn't convinced and gave me half a cereal bar, saying I might have low blood sugar. I was really irritated by her proffered diagnosis, but I think she meant well. I accepted the food graciously and she and her partner walked on.

Having vertigo forces me to take things more slowly. The advantage of this is that I can appreciate what is around me more. Every little detail stands out in technicolour. I thought there was very little that I didn't notice. On the side of the wall, one brick had partially crumbled. A yellow flowering weed was growing there, together with some moss. It looked like a fairy alcove. Someone had left a coin there, a Kuna, no doubt. On closer inspection, I realised it was a medieval coin, roughly hewn and with an unfamiliar figure on one side. I thought it best to leave it there for good luck. I didn't want to make the fairies angry. Life was hard enough without provoking their wrath.

I walked about a mile and decided to make my descent via another set of steps. This wasn't easy and I had to take it very slow. What with vast wings attached to my back and the massive roots growing from my feet to steady me, I was a little encumbered as I walked, step by step, onto street level. I must say the people behind me were very patient and didn't rush me at all. I was grateful for their understanding.

The first thing I did was head for a restaurant in a side street away from the crowds. I found a quiet place with few customers. I ordered soup, though I still felt nauseous. I managed to keep the spicy liquid and olive bread down, but only just. I thought it best to make my way to the coach stop and go back to the hotel. I'd had enough exposure therapy for one day. No more heights for me for a while. I could go out again in the evening if I felt better.

Back in familiar surroundings, I saw Miss Marple sunning herself by the pool that was in the pretty garden forecourt of the building. Plinths with urns full of flowers surrounded the area, and my elderly friend in her white chiffon kaftan and chunky gold necklace looked like a Grecian goddess. I waved, but she seemed a million miles away, facing heavenward.

I changed into my swimming costume and wrapped a kimono-style robe around me. After quickly applying some make-up, not to be outdone by my glamorous acquaintance, I made it poolside in time to see her wake from slumber.

"Oh, it's you," she said, curling her lip in a friendly smile.

"Yes, I'm afraid Dubrovnik's great wall proved to be a step too far for me. I have vertigo, you see." I removed my robe and descended the steps into the water. We were the only two here by the pool, the other residents must have been on the beach or on some exciting excursion.

"Poor you," she said. "My nephew suffered that affliction. He was devastated he couldn't fly a plane. Went into finance instead, like my husband." Ah, so now I was learning more about her. That was good. I swam a few short lengths while she looked on.

"I've been out here all morning," she said. "It was awfully dull until you arrived."

"You missed the deluge, then?"

"What deluge?" she asked.

"Around 10.45. Luckily I was sheltering under awnings at the time. A wedding party was soaked. Totally ruined their day."

"Wedding party? Deluge? There was no rain here, just clear blue sky without a cloud in sight. But you've reminded me of my wedding day in 1932. We chose Dubrovnik Cathedral as the venue. Cecil insisted we get wed abroad because the weather would be better. But we were drenched to the skin. The downpour was so sudden that we were all taken by surprise. It was most peculiar. I'll never forget it. Cecil and I were mortified. What a start to our marriage!"

I was getting a familiar tingling up my spine.

"Your husband, Cecil, did he wear a monocle by any chance?" I asked.

"Why, yes, how did you know that?" Her face was a picture of puzzlement.

"Oh, just a hunch. I can be a bit psychic on occasion," I replied.

"How marvellous! I wish I could be psychic like that. You must have won the lottery countless times," she said with a sparkle in her eye.

"Sadly, no, not so far. But the sun is shining, the pool is refreshing and I'm in lovely company. I feel like I've won the lottery today," I said before getting out of the water and lying down on a recliner near the lady.

"That's so sweet," she said. "It's the kind of thing my husband would have said to me. He died in the spring of 1972. I never remarried." I felt very odd all of a sudden, as if the day's events hadn't been strange enough. I was born in December 1972 and I felt I had a close connection to this woman, I knew it as soon as I'd seen her at breakfast. Surely it couldn't be that I was Cecil's reincarnation.

"Do you believe in past lives?" I asked her.

"Strange you should ask that. No I don't, but Cecil was a firm believer. After he came back from India he believed in all kinds of extraordinary things."

"He sounds like he was an interesting man," I said.

"He was to me, but terribly vain with it. He didn't like growing old. I'm glad he didn't see me aging. It would have shocked him."

"I think he'd have loved you just the same as always," I told her, and I meant it.

"Perhaps," she said, adjusting her kaftan to cover her legs. "I miss him, you know."

"I bet you do. But love never dies, even if the beloved departs," I remarked, thinking of my recently deceased cat, Tabitha.

"I think you're right. What a wise lady you are. An old soul perhaps?" she enquired, tilting her head thoughtfully to one side.

"Or just one who's had many past lives, perhaps," I said, winking at her.

"Oh, that must be it," she said. "This is my first life, I'm sure of it. Everything is so wondrous and new to me. Even now I take delight in so many things. I'll never tire of life."

"You have such élan," I said.

"That's so funny. Cecil often used to say that very same thing to me." A flash of recognition crossed her face and she burst into tears. After that she held my hand for a long time, and we were silent, appreciating the moment and one another, ages apart but somehow connected. Then she spoke.

"Before he died he said something odd. He told me that once he was gone there would be a wall between us, but that he would be on the other side and one day he would cross it to see me again. I never really knew what he meant until now. I think his spirit is in you, but not you. You have channelled him somehow with your psychic abilities. I sense his presence strongly now."

"I don't feel any different from normal, just a little dizzy. My vertigo often brings on this strange state," I said.

"I think that's the spirits that have gone beyond, trying to communicate with you," she told me, smiling sagely.

"I wonder if you're right," I said.

"The proof is in the pudding," she told me.

"Whatever do you mean?"

"What pudding would you like now if you could have any on earth?"

"Profiteroles," I said with mysterious certainty, though I don't know why because I wasn't a fan of that chocolaty dessert.

"His favourite!" she cried. And we laughed. Somehow the laughter caused my dizziness to lift and the strange state I was in evaporated. She let go of my hand.

"I think he's gone now, back to the other side of the wall. But thank you for bringing him to me again. We must meet up again when I return to London. I love the ballet. I can get us tickets. I have a friend whose daughter works at the box office for the Royal Ballet."

"That would be splendid," I said. "Though I usually spend evenings child-minding, I can make an exception."

"I'm glad you will because this is one hell of an exceptional situation."

I agreed.

Back in London I never heard from my Miss Marple again though I had given her my number. Her name, as she told me before we parted ways, was actually Eloise McGovern. When I looked her up on the internet I discovered she had been a well-known dancer in younger days. Then, sadly, I found her obituary. But it stated she had died on 21st September 2003, exactly one year before I supposedly met her in the hotel in Dubrovnik. I was startled by this news and thought it must be another Eloise McGovern, but no, her picture below the obit proved it was the same lady. Apparently she died on the steps of the cathedral in which she married her beloved Cecil in 1932, at the age of 95. She'd had a stroke. It was instant. I'm glad she didn't suffer.

I often think of Eloise. I hope she has transited over the wall to meet her Cecil by now and they are together again. I'm glad she turned up in my world, though, and I hope I live with as much élan as she did. I want to still have that quality in the world beyond the wall, whatever that might be. I no longer fear death. Instead I worry about not living life to the full in the time I have left. I'm not planning a return trip to Dubrovnik any time soon. I will leave those visits to the great Mrs McGovern, if she still chooses to go there in years to come. I picture her, by the pool, goddess-like and calm, looking heavenward at a clear blue sky of infinite beauty. Then I see her rising up on a cloud, dancing gracefully in her white kaftan, to meet with Cecil, in top hat and tails, as they ascend the stairway to paradise together, arm in arm.

Printed in Great Britain
by Amazon

15182591R00061